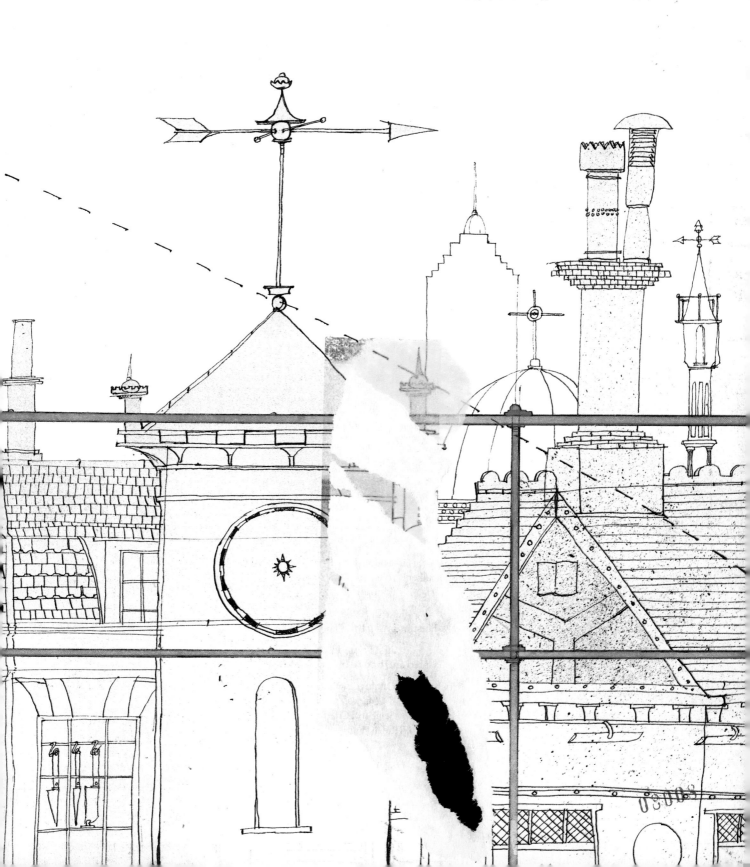

For Eddie and Sam Hadley

J.M.

For Amelia

D.H.

First published 1989 by
Walker Books Ltd, 87 Vauxhall Walk
London SE11 5HJ

Text © 1989 Jan Mark
Illustrations © 1989 David Hughes

First Printed 1989
Printed and bound by Grafedit, Italy

British Library Cataloguing in Publication Data
Mark, Jan
Strat and Chatto
I. Title II. Hughes, David
823'.914 [J] PZ7

ISBN 0-7445-1107-0

STRAT AND CHATTO

Written by
Jan Mark

Illustrated by
David Hughes

WALKER BOOKS
LONDON

A rat ran up the fire escape and rapped at the cat flap.

A cat looked out. His name was Chatto and it was his flap.

"Good morning," said the rat, with his tail over his arm. "I hear you have a mouse problem. Can I be of assistance?"

"I certainly have a problem," said Chatto. "However, excuse my mentioning it, but aren't you of the mouse class yourself?"

"I am a rat," said the rat, "and you may call me Strat – short for Stratorat. I'm a high-flyer." He tried to look modest but his whiskers twitched.

"Oh, a bat," said the cat.

"No, a rat," said Strat. "But some of my best friends are bats," he added. "We hang around together."

"Do you live in the belfry?" Chatto said.

"No," Strat said, "I have a pad in that place over there."

"The place where it says CONDEMNED on the door?" Chatto said. "That's a funny name for a house."

"It means 'Beautiful View' in Latin," Strat said. "Now, about these mice."

"One mouse," said Chatto. "I've eaten the others but this one eludes me. It sits on the fridge and drops lentils on my head."

"Let's have a dekko," said Strat, and he climbed through the cat flap.

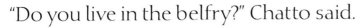

Chatto lived in a good clean kitchen with many corners and cracks in the floor.

"This is a bit of all right," said Strat. "I've always fancied a pad in a flat."

"Hallo, Blotto," said a voice from high up.

"That's him," said Chatto. "That's my mouse. He pretends he doesn't know my name."

A lentil fell on his head.

Strat sprang onto the swing bin for a better view. The mouse lay at ease on top of the fridge with a pile of lentils beside him. He leaned on one elbow and yawned. "Poor old Blotto," he said. "Fratting with rats now, are we? How low can you sink?"

He dropped another lentil.

"That is surely a problem mouse," said Strat. "Give me a day to think about it."

"Can you get him out?" Chatto asked.

"Fat chance," said the mouse.

"Leave it to Strat," said the rat. "I have influence in high places." He ran back down the fire escape to his house, the one with CONDEMNED on the door.

That night Strat climbed to the belfry
and yelled at the bats.

"Belt up," said the eldest bat.

"Ah, come on, now," said Strat. "You'd do
a favour for an old mate, wouldn't you?"

"What would we have to do?".
asked the dangling bats.

"Only what you're doing now,"
said Strat, "but somewhere else, no sweat.
A change is as good as a feast. I'd like
you to spend a few nights with
a friend of mine, but don't
tell him I sent you."

"Where do we find this friend?"
said the eldest bat.

"He lives at the top of the fire escape,"
said Strat. "It's easy to get in.
There's a bat flap."

Next day Strat ran up the fire escape. Chatto came out.

"How's tricks?" said Strat.

"Worse and worse," said Chatto. "Now I have bats hanging from the cup hooks."

"Give me a day to think about it," said Strat. "I have friends in low places," and he ran down the fire escape.

That night Strat went to the kitchen
of the Corner Cafe where cockroaches
feasted in the grease beneath the cooker.

"Fancy a change of fat?" said Strat, to a lurking roach.

"What for?" said the cockroach.

"I hear tell there's a man coming with a can of bane to
spray you with," said Strat. "Better move on till he's gone."

"Where shall we go?" asked the cockroach, quivering.

"Turn right at the fire escape," said Strat. "A friend of
mine will put you up."

"Thanks for the tip," the cockroach said.

"Think nothing of it, pal," said Strat.

"We vermin must stick together.

Enjoy yourselves, there are

plenty of lentils."

VINTAGE
Greece

SWE
V

1982

6

WINE
MEDIUM GREASE

DRY GREASE

MYTHICAL GREECE

ANTIFREEZE
GREE

LE MENU
GREASE KEBAB
GREAS ALIVE
GREASE 'N V
SAUCE
FLUFF N'GRA

Next day Strat ran up the fire escape and out came Chatto.

"Fine help you've been," Chatto snapped. "Now I have cockroaches loafing in the corners and bats hanging from the cup hooks, not to mention lentils in my ears."

"Give me a day to think about it," said Strat, and he ran down the fire escape.

That night Strat crept to the ingle nook in the public bar of the Rook and Parsnip, and fetched out the silverfish.

"Fancy a change of furnace?" said Strat.

"What for?" said the silverfish.

"I know a place that offers weekend breaks for people like you," said Strat. "There's a nice warm boiler and luxury cracks in the floor. Pop along tomorrow and don't say I sent you."

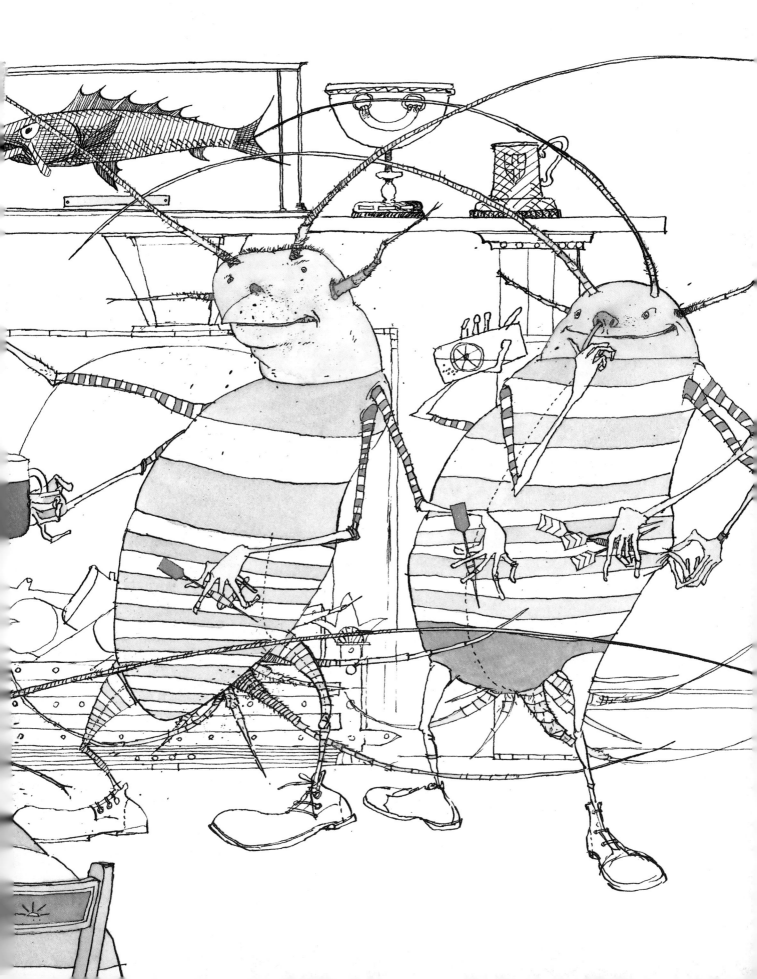

Next day Strat ran up the fire escape and Chatto sprang out of the cat flap.

"When are you going to act?" cried Chatto. "I have bats on the cup hooks, cockroaches in the corners and sixty-five silverfish slithering about in the cracks. I counted them in. Also," he said, "that low-down mouse is still dropping lentils on my head from a great height."

"Give me a day to think about it," said Strat, and he ran down the fire escape.

Next morning he met a toad in the road.

"Come with me," said Strat. "I know someone who ought to meet you."

He ran up the fire escape with the toad at his heels. Out came Chatto like a bar of wet soap and screamed, "DO SOMETHING!"

"Hang about," said Strat. "I'd like you to meet my loathsome friend."

Chatto took one look at the toad and moaned, "I can't stand it." He fell flat on the fire escape and put his paws over his eyes.